Illustrated by Russ Daff

W

Dev and Amber had a new game.
They were getting their horses
ready for a show.

"I've got some oats for Shadow!"

shouted Dev.

"I've got a whistle for Bouncer!"

yelled Amber.

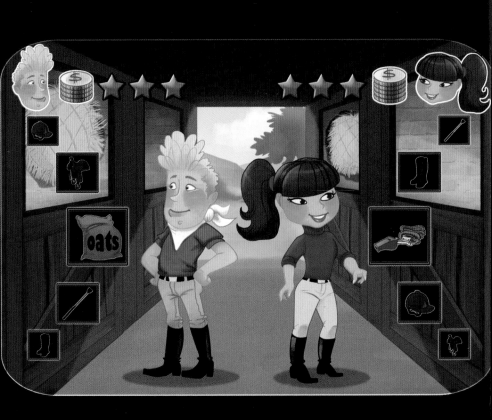

Suddenly, a red light shone ...

Dev and Amber were at the stables!

"Where are we?" asked Amber.

6

"I think we're in the game!" said Dev.

"Look, there's Bouncer!"

A groom ran up, panting.

"Have you seen the horses?" he asked.

"Just Bouncer, but he ran off," said Dev.

The groom groaned. "The gate was left open. If we don't find the horses soon, there will be no show!"

Soon the stables were full of people.

"Quick! We must find the horses!

We have an hour!" the groom shouted.

"Bouncer went that way," said Amber.

"That goes to the beach!" said Dev.

"Shadow loves it there."

Down at the beach, Dev and Amber

got a shock.

The horses were there, but they
were trapped by the tide.

"This way!" said Dev. He ran over the dunes to the other side of the beach. "They can get up here," he said.

Dev and Amber shouted loudly.
But the horses could not hear
them over the crashing waves.

"The whistle!" Amber cried.

She blew as hard as she could.

Bouncer's ears pricked up. He cantered towards her. Shadow followed Bouncer. Then all the horses followed.

"Good boy, Bouncer!" said Amber. "Now how do we get the horses to follow us?"

Dev smiled. "I've got the oats!"

he said. "Shadow won't mind sharing."

"Good idea," laughed Amber.

Everyone cheered as they walked in.

"Thank you!" said the groom.

"Can you come to our show?"

But before Dev and Amber could reply, a red light shone ...

... and they were back home.

"That was a brilliant game!"

they laughed.

PUZZLE TIME

a

b

Can you put these pictures

in the correct order?

TURN OVER FOR ANSWERS!

Tell the story in your own words

with YOU as the hero!

ANSWERS

The correct order is: b, d, a, c.

First published in 2011 by
Franklin Watts
338 Euston Road
London
NW1 3BH

Franklin Watts Australia
Level 17/207 Kent Street
Sydney
NSW 2000

Text © Jack D. Clifford 2011
Illustration © Russ Daff 2011

The rights of Jack D. Clifford to be
identified as the author and Russ Daff
as the illustrator of this Work have been
asserted in accordance with the Copyright,
Designs and Patents Act, 1988.

A CIP catalogue record for this book is
available from the British Library.

ISBN 978 1 4451 0305 1 (hbk)
ISBN 978 1 4451 0313 6 (pbk)

Series Editor: Jackie Hamley
Series Advisor: Catherine Glavina
Series Designer: Peter Scoulding

Printed in China

Franklin Watts is a division of Hachette
Children's Books, an Hachette UK company.
www.hachette.co.uk